I0618094

Lela
&
Her Magic Bank of Dreams

Authored By: K. Nicole Smith

To my William and Lela,

May your reach always
exceed your grasp.

Dream Big!

Lela was a girl with BIG dreams.

She dreamed of the magic of far away lands in Japan...

...the mystery of the mountains in Peru...

...and the colors of the canyons in America.

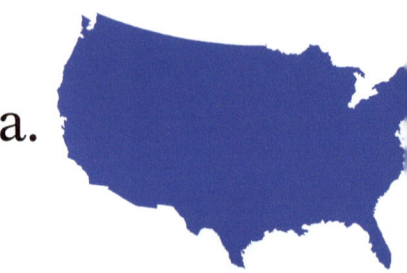

She wished for the adventure of the great outdoors
in Argentina...

...the golden sands of the pyramids in Egypt...

...and the echoes of the whispering waterfalls in Brazil.

After school, she loved to read about the secrets of the deep blue sea in Australia.

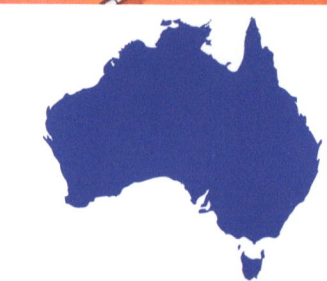

"Teddy, I wish all of my dreams would come true," said Lela one night.

Suddenly, her piggy bank started to shimmer and shake.
A genie appeared!
"Every dollar you get, put into this magic dream bank
and one day all of your dreams will come true," said
the genie.

"All of my dreams?" said Lela.
"All of your dreams!" said the genie.

Lela woke up to find money under her
pillow from the tooth fairy.
She put it in her magic dream bank!

After a perfect score on her spelling test, Lela's parents gave her money.
She put it in her magic dream bank!

Lela earned money delivering newspapers.
She put it in her magic dream bank!

One day while walking home from school, Lela saw the shiniest pair of shoes she had ever seen.

"Aren't the shoes beautiful? They can be yours for just $20!" said the shopkeeper.

"I have $20 in my magic dream bank!" exclaimed Lela.

Lela ran home to get the money.

When she opened her magic dream bank, she saw ALL of her dreams in front of her...

...dreams of climbing the highest glaciers in Iceland...

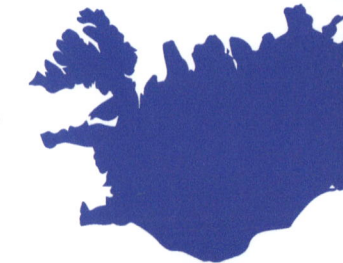

...dreams of ziplining through the wildest jungles of New Zealand...

...and dreams of skiing down the snow-covered hills of Canada.

"I like the shoes, but my dreams are way bigger," thought Lela as she closed her magic dream bank.

Lela kept saving,
Lela kept dreaming.

The bank grew and grew.
It grew so big, it began to crack!

Lela earned money for helping her grandfather paint.
She stuffed the money in the magic dream bank.

The bank exploded!!

Lela found herself in the far away lands of
Austria...

...marvelling at floating lanterns in Thailand...

...amazed in Rooms of Rainbows in Spain...

...and walking along the brightest bays of Puerto Rico.

Lela saved so much that all of her dreams came true!

The End

ALASKA (USA)

GREENLAND (DENMARK)

ICELAND

C A N A D A

UNITED STATES OF AMERICA

AZORES (PORTUGAL)

MEXICO

THE BAHAMAS

CUBA

SAINT KITTS AND NEVIS

ANTIGUA AND BARBUDA

DOMINICA

MARTINIQUE

SAINT LUCIA

SAINT VINCENT

BARBADOS

TRINIDAD AND TOBAGO

BELIZE

GUATEMALA

HONDURAS

EL SALVADOR

NICARAGUA

COSTA RICA

PANAMA

VENEZUELA

COLOMBIA

GUYANA

SURINAME

FRENCH GUIANA

ECUADOR

B R A Z I L

PERU

BOLIVIA

PARAGUAY

CHILE

URUGUAY

ARGENTINA

FALKLAND ISLANDS (UK)

SOUTH GEORGIA (UK)

Dream Big!

designed by freepik.com

www.ingramcontent.com/pod-product-compliance
Lightning Source LLC
Chambersburg PA
CBHW041003170626
46815CB00002B/131